PONY ISLAND

Candice F. Ransom

illustrated by Wade Zahares

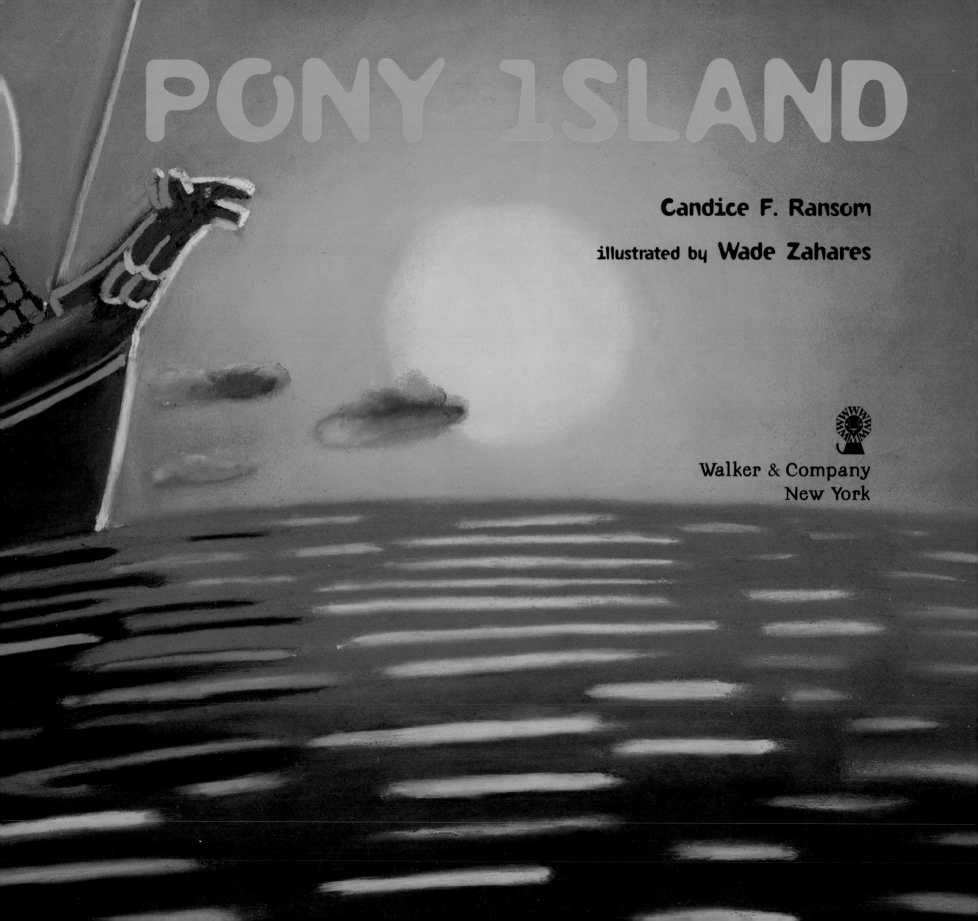

Walker & Company
New York

Big ship wrecks.

Stormy sea.

Cargo horses

Swimming free.

Churning water.
Cannot wade.
Struggling horses—
Lost, afraid.

Empty island.
Room to roam.
Birds and beaches.
Brand-new home.

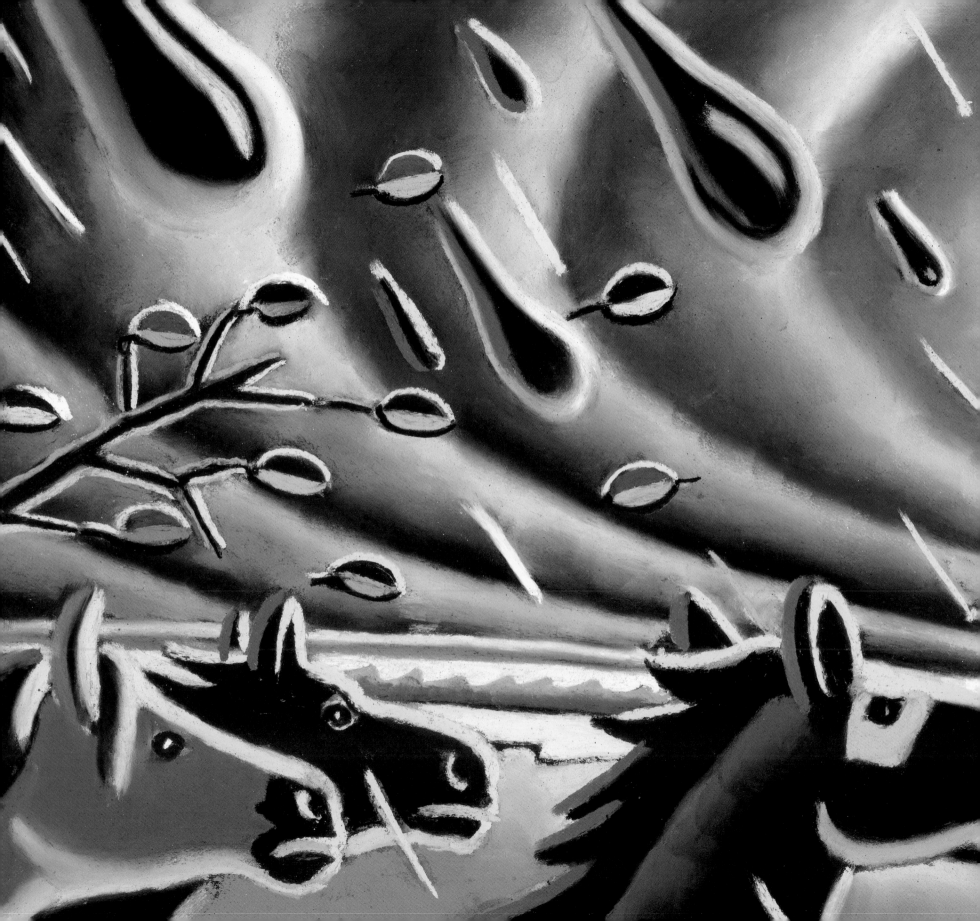

Nature's fury.
Hurricanes.
Wind and lightning.
Soaking rains.

Meager forage.

Frozen oats.

Winter blizzard.

Shaggy coats.

Snow geese journey
Spring and fall.
Island horses
Now are small.

Neighbor island.

Settlers stay.

Town grows, men work.

Ocean, bay.

Clam beds, crab pots.
Oysters, trout.
Rowboat, dinghy,
Runabout.

Blazing rooftop.
Sound alarm!
Pets and people
Run from harm.

Fire leaps from
House to house.
Buckets, hoses.
Cannot douse.

Firemen meeting.

Must raise cash.

Need new pumper

In a flash!

Pony island.
Round 'em up.
Crack whips, flap hats.
Giddyap!

Stragglers ready.
Check the tide.
Stick not moving.
Cowboys ride!

Swim the channel,
Noses high.
Ponies dripping.
Crowd stands by.

Stallions, mares
Race through town.
Nicker, whinny.
Black and brown.

People circle
Pony pen.

Yearlings, colts sell.

Six, eight, ten!

Happy children.
Starry eyes.
Own a pony
Just their size.

Island ponies
Swim back home.
Cowboys leave them
Safe to roam.

Shiny engine.
People cheer.
Bring back ponies
Every year!

Morning sunrise
By the sea.
Ponies gallop,
Wild and free.

AUTHOR'S NOTE

Chincoteague ponies actually live on Assateague, a barrier island off the coasts of Maryland and Virginia. Chincoteague lies between Assateague and the Virginia mainland. As a longtime visitor to Chincoteague, I have fallen under the spell of the island and its wild ponies.

The ponies' origin is a mystery. One legend says the ponies were castaways from a Spanish shipwreck. Another story claims pirates left their horses on the island to graze, planning to return later to pick them up. Historians believe Chincoteague settlers moved their free-roaming horses to Assateague to sort and brand them. The farmers also moved their horses to Assateague to avoid paying livestock taxes, and some horses stayed on the island. "Teagers," as Chincoteague islanders are called, prefer the shipwreck legend. However it happened, the ponies arrived about four hundred years ago and grew smaller as they adapted to harsh life on the windswept island.

Although some Chincoteague horses had occasionally been penned on Assateague over the years, the Chincoteague Volunteer Fire Department held the first official Pony Penning and Firemen's Carnival in 1925 to raise money for a new pumper truck. On July 30, 1925, "saltwater cowboys" rounded up the wild herds on Assateague and drove them across the channel to Chincoteague to be sold, earning the fire company more than $6,000.

Pony penning became an annual event. Marguerite Henry made the island and its ponies famous with her book *Misty of Chincoteague*. A movie about Misty was filmed on the island in 1961.

Today, 75,000 visitors flock to Chincoteague during the last week of July to watch the ponies make the five-minute swim at "slack" tide, which is determined when a stick tossed in the water stops moving.

Though the ponies remain wild, the Chincoteague Volunteer Fire Company cares for the Virginia herd (the ponies on the Maryland half of Assateague are part of the National Wildlife Refuge). The firemen feed the ponies and bring food and water during heavy snows. Three times a year the ponies are checked by veterinarians.

Whether the ponies swam to Assateague from a wrecked ship, were left on the island by pirates, or escaped from the herds brought over by Chincoteague farmers, they are the stars of Chincoteague Island's biggest event. The rest of the year, they live as they have for centuries—wild and free.

FOR FURTHER READING AND SURFING

BOOKS

Arnosky, Jim. *Wild Ponies*. One Whole Day. Washington DC: National Geographic Books, 2002.

Henry, Marguerite. *Misty of Chincoteague*. New York: Aladdin, 2006.

Jeffers, Susan. *My Chincoteague Pony*. New York: Hyperion, 2008.

Lockhart, Lynne N., and Barbara M. Lockhart. *Once a Pony Time at Chincoteague*. Maryland: Tidewater Publishers, 1992.

Wilcox, Charlotte. *The Chincoteague Pony*. Learning about Horses. Minnesota: Capstone Press, 1996.

WEB SITES

www.ansi.okstate.edu/breeds/horses

www.chincoteague.com/pony/ponies.html

www.pony-chincoteague.org/chincoteague-pony-info.html

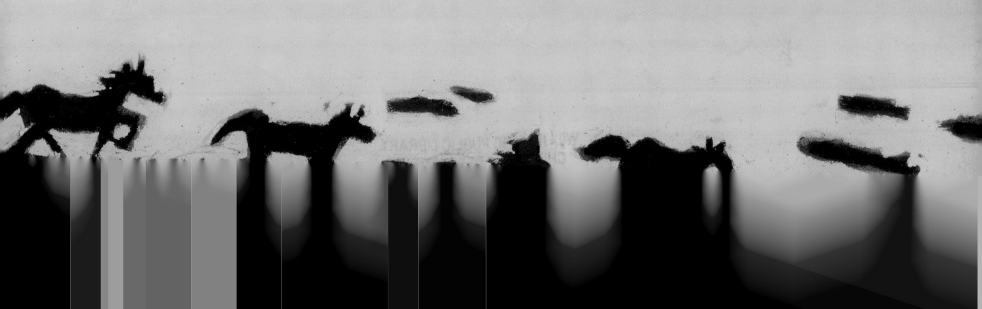

To Taylor, Sherri, Ashley, and Alex —C. F. R.

For Kim, Sara, and Isabella —W. Z.

First published in the United States of America in 2009 by Walker Publishing Company, Inc.
Visit Walker & Company's Web site at www.walkeryoungreaders.com

For information about permission to reproduce selections from this book, write to
Permissions, Walker & Company, 175 Fifth Avenue, New York, New York 10010

Library of Congress Cataloging-in-Publication Data
Ransom, Candice F.
Pony island / Candice F. Ransom ; illustrated by Wade Zahares.
p.   cm.
Summary: Rhyming text describes the origins of Chincoteague ponies and how they were rounded
up and sold for the first time to pay for a new fire engine. Includes facts about the ponies, their
home on Assateague island, and their relationship with the people of Chincoteague island.
ISBN-13: 978-0-8027-8088-1 • ISBN-10: 0-8027-8088-1 (hardcover)
ISBN-13: 978-0-8027-8089-8 • ISBN-10: 0-8027-8089-X (reinforced)
1. Chincoteague pony—Juvenile fiction. [1. Chincoteague pony—Fiction. 2. Ponies—Fiction.
3. Chincoteague Island (Va)—Fiction. 4. Assateague Island (Md. and Va)—Fiction]
I. Zahares, Wade, ill. II. Title.
PZ10.3.R176Pon 2009   [E]—dc22   2008013356

Typeset in Andromeda
Illustrations are pastel on paper

Printed in China
2 4 6 8 10 9 7 5 3 1 (hardcover)
2 4 6 8 10 9 7 5 3 1 (reinforced)